Vanessa and Frankie Baldacci have produced lots of historical adventures for you to enjoy, including *The Victorian Time Traveller, Frederick Ramsbottom's WW2 Adventure* and *The Victorian and FBI Agents.*

These books have been derived with Frankie's incredible creative imagination and his mum, Vanessa Baldacci, is very proud of him. This is a huge achievement as Frankie struggles with severe learning difficulties daily which affects his cognitive development. Now having more confidence in himself, he hopes to inspire other children from all walks of life.

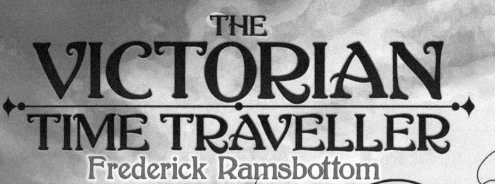

THE VICTORIAN TIME TRAVELLER

Frederick Ramsbottom

Vanessa Baldacci
and
Frankie Baldacci

AUSTIN MACAULEY PUBLISHERS™

LONDON • CAMBRIDGE • NEW YORK • SHARJAH

A CIP catalogue record for this title is available from the British Library.

ISBN 9781398426955 (Paperback)
ISBN 9781398426962 (ePub e-book)

www.austinmacauley.com

First Published 2021
Austin Macauley Publishers Ltd®
1 Canada Square
Canary Wharf
London
E14 5AA

This book is dedicated to my Nan and Grandad, Jean and Francesco Baldacci, who are my greatest heroes and whom I love very much.

I would like to give a big thank you to all my school teachers at Cavendish – Trinity School & College, especially to Mrs Beswick, Miss Sargeant and Mrs Baines, who have inspired me to use my creative skills.

Frederick Ramsbottom is a time traveller. He's a Victorian chap.
With the magical telephone box, crystals and aerials, he makes a time machine.
Frederick presses the buttons, the door opens, and he goes inside. He shuts the door. He pulls the lever, presses the buttons and **WHOOSHHH** magically disappears in the night sky.

To Frederick Ramsbottom's
amazement, he has teleported to
the Roman Times.
He looks around very curiously,
making sure no one has spotted him.

Before leaving The Magical Time Machine, Frederick makes it invisible by pointing his neon ring worn on his pinky finger which creates an auto invisible shield as he doesn't want the Romans to find it.

He runs towards the Roman Castle
making his way over the ancient bridge.

He climbs the Roman Castle using a Teleportation Compass Bracelet made with a leather strap and a round compass face with one button on either side. The compass symbols denote the direction for travelling: NORTH, EAST, SOUTH or WEST and each button has a function. The first button once pressed shoots out strong wired string to climb high buildings and the second button releases a transparent liquid in a shape of a crystal to teleport on.

Frederick reaches the very top of the castle and climbs in, noticing that the Roman Emperor was in residence and being guarded by Roman Guards.

He finds all of the shiny gold swords
and jewels sparkling like stars from
a night's sky. He carefully places
them all in a bag and leaves the
building without making a sound.

SHHHHHH...

He presses the button on the
Teleportation Compass Bracelet to
release transparent liquid crystal
to teleport him to the ground.

WHOOSHHH

Frederick runs to the time machine, pointing his neon ring worn on his pinky finger to unleash the auto invisible shield. The Magical Time Machine appears before his very eyes; he pushes the door, rushes in and shuts the door firmly.
A Roman Guard spots him and shouts for help.

The Time Machine is surrounded
by Roman Guards.

They manage to open The Magical
Time Machine door to Frederick
Ramsbottom's amazement.
With Frederick's quick thinking,
he remembers he had a specially
adapted Victorian Pocket Watch
which beams out a bright laser
flash of light. The light is so bright,
all the Guards stand back, covering
their faces with their Scutum Shield.

The door shuts tight, purple lights flash, **WHOOSHHH** and Frederick is teleported back to London.
The Roman Guards all look astonished with puzzled expressions on their faces.
URGHHH

One of the Roman Guards gets sucked into the teleportation!
SH-LOOP

He lands in dirty old London
in Frederick's warehouse.
The warehouse is very big and safe
to keep The Magical Time Machine
hidden from any prying eyes or unwanted
attention as these magical machines and
devices need to be kept secret.

The Guard becomes scared as
Ramsbottom puts on a mask which makes
the Roman run into the town. A Victorian
Police Bobby chases him with hands held
high in the air, angrily shouting,
"Stop that man!"
They have a fight and the Roman Guard
is arrested and taken to a dreary
cold dungeon.

Frederick Ramsbottom has now
become a very rich chap and buys a big
Victorian Mansion in London with secret
underground caves ready to return for
more historical teleportation adventures.

CPSIA information can be obtained
at www.ICGtesting.com
Printed in the USA
LVHW072346061221
705433LV00021BA/3783